Race to the South Pole

KATE MESSNER

illustrated by
KELLEY McMORRIS

Scholastic Press / New York

Library of Congress Cataloging-in-Publication Data
Messner, Kate, author.
Race to the South Pole / Kate Messner ; illustrated by Kelley McMorris.
pages cm. — (Ranger in time)
Summary: Once again the mysterious box takes the golden retriever Ranger
back in time, and he finds himself on Robert Falcon Scott's ship, the *Terra
Nova*, headed for Antarctica, where his mission is to save Jack Nin, a Chinese-
Maori stowaway from New Zealand, from the blizzards, unstable ice, and the
other hazards that lie ahead for the doomed expedition.
1. British Antarctic ("Terra Nova") Expedition (1910–1913) — Juvenile fiction.
2. Golden retriever — Juvenile fiction. 3. Time travel — Juvenile fiction.
4. Adventure stories. 5. Antarctica — Discovery and exploration — Juvenile
fiction. 6. South Pole — Juvenile fiction. [1. British Antarctic ("Terra Nova")
Expedition (1910–1913) — Fiction. 2. Golden retriever — Fiction. 3. Dogs —
Fiction. 4. Time travel — Fiction. 5. Adventure and adventurers — Fiction.
6. Explorers — Fiction. 7. Antarctica — Discovery and exploration — Fiction.
8. South Pole — Discovery and exploration — Fiction.] I. McMorris, Kelley,
illustrator. II. Title. III. Series: Messner, Kate. Ranger in time.
PZ10.3.M5635Rac 2016
813.6 — dc23 2015028421

ISBN 978-0-545-63926-2

10 9 8 7 6 5 4 3 2 1   16 17 18 19 20

Printed in the United States of America   113
First printing 2016

Book design by Ellen Duda

For all the Teachers-Write campers,
Write bravely!

Chapter 1

STOWAWAY!

November 29, 1910

Jack Nin packed the wooden crate with potatoes and cabbages. He loaded it into a cart and hitched up his horse, Whetu. Then they started up the path along the New Zealand coast.

"It's a short journey to Port Chalmers. There, we will sell our goods to the polar explorers," Jack said. "They will leave for the South Pole with Nin family vegetables in the ship's hold!"

Whetu gave a whinny. Jack leaned forward and stroked the star-shaped patch between the horse's eyes. The name Whetu meant "star" in Maori, the language of Jack's mother. But Jack and his brothers rarely spoke that language aloud. They didn't speak Chinese outside of the house, either. Jack's father had insisted on English. Being half Maori and half Chinese already brought enough trouble.

Jack's father had died a year ago. Now his mother struggled to run the family's market garden with her four boys. They sold their potatoes, cabbages, tomatoes, and onions to the Chinese greengrocers in Dunedin. But the Nins were struggling. Some people in New Zealand said that Chinese men like Jack's father had stolen their jobs. They urged their neighbors not to do business with Chinese market gardeners. Jack hoped the explorers would buy the vegetables he'd brought. Every little bit helped.

When Jack arrived at the harbor, a big ship was tied to the docks. Dogs yapped and howled. Men loaded sacks of coal and tugged ponies into stalls on the deck.

"Excuse me," Jack called to a man carrying a sack over his shoulder. "Are you from the ship?"

"I am," the man said. He had brown hair and a stubble of beard.

"Might you purchase goods for your journey? My family has the finest vegetables you'll find in Dunedin." Jack pulled a folded-up piece of paper from his pocket. He'd made a sign for the Nin market garden, with drawings to show all of the vegetables. Sketching felt like magic to Jack. He loved filling blank paper with objects that looked real enough to touch.

"Perhaps some potatoes or cabbages?" Jack said.

The man laughed. "We're headed to Antarctica, my friend. It's a five-week voyage to the continent, and who knows how many more before we reach the South Pole. Fresh vegetables won't keep. We need our space for biscuits and pemmican — dried beef and fat that'll last far longer than your cabbages."

"Of course," Jack said. How foolish he was not to realize that.

"But . . ." the man went on. His eyes had a lively sparkle as he shifted the sack to his other shoulder. "We may be interested in some of your goods for a feast before we depart. Wait here." The man carried his load to the ship and returned with some money.

Jack unloaded his crate from the horse cart and accepted the coins. "Thank you," he said. He knew he should start for home. There was work to be done. But he couldn't stop star-ing at the tall-masted ship. It buzzed with activity and adventure. "You think you'll reach the pole?"

"I'm sure of it." The man grinned. "You'll see my name in the newspaper when we return. Apsley Cherry-Garrard, right along with the famous Captain Scott."

Jack imagined what it would be like to travel to a place no one had ever seen. It made him think of his grandfather, who'd come to New Zealand to work in the Otago gold mines as a young man so he could send money to his family in China. Jack wished he could help his mother that way. But the mines had been cleared of their gold long ago.

Jack looked at the big ship and wondered if there might be another way to help. "Do you need more workers?" he asked.

The man shook his head. "Thousands came forward when Captain Scott put out his call for workers. I was lucky to be chosen myself."

The man looked back at the ship. "When we depart, we'll be a crew of sixty-five men, along with thirty-three dogs and nineteen ponies to pull the sleds."

"I see. Thank you, then." Jack turned back to his horse. He couldn't stop thinking about his grandfather's courage, setting off for a new land to help his family.

And he couldn't stop thinking about his own whanau.

Whanau is "family" in Maori, but it was more than Jack's mother and brothers. It was his extended family and the spirits of his ancestors. Jack had a responsibility to all of them.

What if he snuck onto the ship and hid until it was far from port? He could show Captain Scott and the others what a strong worker he was. Surely, they would accept him as a cabin boy. Then he could earn money for his family.

His brothers could manage the market garden without him for a time. And while he was gone, his mother would have one less mouth to feed. He would return home in a few weeks — or months, perhaps? Jack didn't know how long it might take to get to the South Pole after they reached land. But the longer he soaked up the excitement at the harbor, the more he wanted to go.

Jack searched the crowd until he spotted a familiar face.

"Pak Keung!" Jack called. The boy was a little younger than Jack, the son of one of the greengrocers who did business with the Nin family, so he and Jack had become friends. Jack took a coin from his pocket and held it up. "I have a job that I must do. Will you take Whetu home for me? Tell my mother I am going on a trip, to earn money that will help our family."

The boy agreed, accepted the coin, and took Whetu's reins.

"Give these to my mother," Jack said, and handed the boy the rest of the coins. "Tell her there will be more when I return."

Then, Jack headed for the pile of coal sacks being loaded onto the boat. He hoisted one over his shoulder. It was heavy, but Jack was strong from hauling vegetables. He went straight to the boat, as if he'd been hired to carry coal like the other men. But when Jack tossed the sack onto the deck, he didn't return to shore. He slipped past the coal sacks to the pony stalls. When no one was watching, he ducked behind a crate of horse feed.

Jack crouched low and still. He waited for what must have been more than an hour. His legs cramped. Every time someone walked by, his heart jumped into his throat.

Finally, the ship's great horn gave a blast.

Jack peered out from behind the crate. The explorers kissed their wives good-bye and waved them back to shore. The band played. The crowd cheered. And the *Terra Nova* pulled away from the dock.

Chapter 2

SNOWBALLS AND SQUIRRELS

"Ranger, catch!" Luke packed a big snowball and tossed it high over the yard.

Ranger bounded through the new snow, leaped into the air, and caught it in his teeth. He chomped down, and the snowball exploded in pieces. Some of them stuck in Ranger's fur.

"Ranger has a beard!" Sadie laughed. "You look like Grandpa," she said, and brushed the fluffy white snow off Ranger's chin with her mitten.

Just then, Ranger caught a scent. *Squirrel!*

There it was, underneath Mom's bird feeder! Ranger took off running, but the squirrel raced through the snow and up a tree.

Ranger barked up at it.

Luke laughed. "Poor Ranger. Missed another one."

Ranger loved chasing squirrels more than almost anything. They were the reason he failed his test to become a search-and-rescue dog, even though he'd done all of the training. To be a search-and-rescue dog, you had to ignore squirrels, even when they were right there, giving off their wonderful, swishy-tailed smells right under your nose! Ranger chased them every time. If a real person needed help, he knew he'd be able to follow directions, but that wasn't good enough for the search-and-rescue trainers, so Ranger didn't get to go on any real searches.

He'd had lots of practice searching and

rescuing, though. He'd searched for people in the muggy woods of summer and sniffed out people in the slush and ice of winter. Ranger could find a scent even when the person was buried in snow. Sometimes, his paws got icy during winter training. Ranger liked summer searches better.

"I'm getting cold," Luke said. "Want to go in for some hot cocoa?"

"And cookies!" Sadie said. "I'll race you to the house."

Ranger didn't drink cocoa, but he was ready to go inside. Also, he loved the cookie pieces that Sadie slipped him under the kitchen table. So Ranger raced, too. His paws sank deep in the new snow, but he stayed by Luke's side all the way to the door. When Luke opened it, the warm air smelled like chocolate. Luke and Sadie's mom set a plate of oatmeal cookies on the table.

"Ready for a snack?" she said.

Luke and Sadie changed out of their snow pants in the mudroom while Ranger got a drink from his water dish. He was just about to follow them to the kitchen when he heard a humming sound coming from his dog bed.

Ranger went to his bed and pawed his blanket out of the way. Beneath it, he found the antique first aid kit he'd dug up in the family garden. The old metal box had made this sound before. Once, it happened when a boy named Sam and his family needed Ranger's help on a long journey. Another time, the box hummed when a boy named Marcus was in trouble in a big arena, far away. And it had also made the sound when a girl named Sarah was about to leave on a long, dangerous trip.

Ranger had helped those children — and

brought back treasures from his time away. He kept them tucked under the blanket in his dog bed. There was a quilt square Sam had given Ranger when they said good-bye, a strange, long leaf from the boy in the arena, and a soft feather from the Sarah girl. Beside those things sat the old metal first aid kit.

And now, the box was humming again.

Ranger nuzzled its worn leather strap over his neck. The humming grew louder, and the box warmed at his throat. At first, Ranger could still hear the sounds of hot chocolate mugs clinking in the kitchen, but soon, the noise from the box was so loud that it drowned out everything else.

Light began to spill from the cracks in the box. White, hot light! It was so bright that Ranger had to close his eyes.

When he opened them, it was raining.

It wasn't home rain, like the kind Ranger watched from the porch swing with Luke and Sadie. This rain was wild, blowing. And the floor under Ranger's paws was moving — lurching back and forth so much he could hardly stand.

The hot chocolate smell from the kitchen was gone. The air here smelled of salt and sea and wind. It smelled of wooden crates, wet animals, and men. It smelled of panic.

"Strap down the fuel!" a man shouted.

"Lower the topsails!" someone else hollered.

"I can help!" called a boy as he hurried over the deck. Ranger caught his scent — a mix of sweat, horses, and hay.

"Watch out!" screamed a man, and a big sack tumbled down from the heap on the deck.

It washed across the deck on a sloshing wave and flew toward Ranger. He jumped out of the way just in time. But the sack knocked the boy's feet out from under him.

Ranger barked.

The boy cried out and disappeared over the side of the boat.

Chapter 3

STORM ON THE *TERRA NOVA*

Ranger raced across the deck. Another wave broke over the rail and swept his paws out from under him. The water sent him sliding over the weathered boards.

Finally, Ranger caught his footing. Where was the boy?

Ranger sniffed the heavy, wet air. It was full of smells. Sea and coal, men and fear.

Ranger made his way across the rocking ship. The scent he was tracking grew stronger.

Ranger looked down. *There!* The boy had caught hold of a thick rope. He was hanging on, swinging over the edge of the ship. Every time it dipped on a wave, his legs plunged into the sea. His hands were raw and red. His eyes were wide with panic.

Ranger barked. In search-and-rescue training, he'd learned to follow a scent to find the person in trouble. Then he barked to give an alert, so Luke and Dad would come. They'd give Ranger hugs and say, "Good dog!" And then they would go home.

This plunging and rocking boat was a long way from home.

Ranger barked again, but no one paid attention. The wind and waves were too loud.

He stumbled over the deck and jumped up on a man who'd bent down to lift a sack.

"Whoa!" The man looked at Ranger, then hollered, "We got another dog loose!" The man lifted his sack and turned away.

Ranger barked a third time. He had given the alert. The boy needed help. Why wasn't the man coming?

Ranger barked and pawed at the deck. The man hurled the sack overboard and turned. "What is it, dog?" He followed Ranger to the far railing.

"Good Lord!" the man said as another wave crashed over the boat. He leaned over the railing, held on with one hand, and extended the other as low as he could. "Grab my hand!" he called down to the boy. A few seconds later, the man leaned back and heaved the boy onto the deck.

The boy coughed, choking on seawater. But he was safe.

Who was he? Ranger looked around the boat. Who were all of these men? Why were they in this windy, wild place?

"I don't know who you are," the man said, pulling the boy to his feet, "but when this gale has passed, the captain will have words with you."

The boy coughed and shivered, but he stood tall. "I'm a good worker," he said.

"You're a child. Hauling coal sacks is a man's work. Stay out of the way."

Jack knew he had to prove himself quickly. He pushed past the man and hoisted a coal sack high above his head. It was heavy, but no more than the vegetable crates he loaded every day. "Does the captain want all the loose sacks overboard?" Jack swayed under the weight as the ship creaked and dipped beneath his feet.

The man looked surprised, but he nodded. "Otherwise, they'll slide around and break loose more important cargo," he said, and went back to work himself.

Jack hurled the sack into the sea and took a moment to catch his breath. He looked down at the dripping golden dog that had probably saved his life. He looked different from the other sled dogs. "Looks like you and I are both outsiders around here." Jack reached down and gave the dog a soggy pat on the head.

"What's that you're carrying?" Jack eased the first aid kit from around Ranger's neck and opened it. "Did someone put you in charge of bandages and things?"

The man from before walked by and heaved another sack of coal into the sea. Then he glanced down at the box in Jack's hands. "That should be with our other supplies. Lord knows we've already lost enough in this storm." He packed Ranger's first aid kit away in one of the crates and turned to Jack. "Get to work now."

All night, Jack worked quietly alongside the men while the waves sloshed over them.

Ranger's fur was soaked and matted. But he stayed by the boy's side. Maybe when the storm ended, he could leave this dizzy, drenched place and go home.

But the wind kept howling. The crew rushed over the deck, retying wooden cases to keep them from washing away. When the biggest waves crashed over the rail, the men clung to posts and ropes. Jack grabbed a mast with one arm and held tight to Ranger with the other.

The ponies stumbled and fell in their stalls. The dogs didn't even have stalls — they were chained together on top of the coal sacks. One had already broken loose and drowned, so a man came and checked all of their chains. He tied Ranger up with the rest of the pack.

Most of the dogs growled at Ranger, sized him up, and then ignored him. But one kept growling and barking at Ranger.

"Settle down, Osman!" one of the crew members hollered.

Osman sat down but never took his eyes off Ranger. Ranger stayed as far away from Osman as his chain allowed.

The coal sacks were lumpy and uncomfortable. Ranger missed his dog bed. He missed Luke.

"We need help in the engine room!" a man yelled. "The pumps are broken, and the water's rising!"

Jack and the other men raced down with buckets and formed a line to bail out their ship.

Most of the men did two-hour shifts, but Jack worked all night and through the next day until the waves died down and the darkness returned. Finally, a man named Evans fixed the pump, and there was great cheering.

When he finished in the engine room, Jack climbed up to find Ranger. Most of the dogs chained on deck were shades of gray and white and black. But the one that had helped him was shaggy and golden.

"Dog!" Jack scrambled over the heap, sat down beside the dog, and petted him on the head. Ranger wagged his dripping tail against the coal sacks.

"Now who do we have here?" A balding man with a serious expression towered over Jack. It was the captain, Jack guessed, from the way he'd commanded the others during the storm.

"My name is Jack Nin." Jack meant to sound brave, but his voice came out small and shaky. "I came aboard in Port Chalmers —"

"Without permission," the captain barked.

Jack looked down. "I did, sir. But I promise that I am a good, strong worker."

"And you hope to be kept on as a cabin boy now, instead of being fed to the sharks?"

Jack nodded and swallowed hard. He'd seen how easily the men tossed coal sacks over the railing. He probably didn't weigh much more than that.

Ranger nuzzled the boy's hand.

The captain looked at Ranger. "This dog isn't part of the sled team. Is he yours?"

"I don't know where he came from, but . . ." Jack looked at the dog. "He saved me when the waves knocked me overboard. So maybe he is my dog. In a way."

"Indeed." The captain sighed. "This has not been the best day at sea. I've lost two ponies, a dog, ten tons of coal, and sixty-five gallons of petrol. And now, I learn that I have a stowaway." The captain shook his head. "But very well," he said. "The men told me how you helped during the gale, and I am thankful.

You shall be our cabin boy. Expect to work hard on this voyage."

Jack's heart leaped higher than the tallest wave. "Yes, sir!"

The captain nodded. "Welcome aboard the *Terra Nova*."

Chapter 4

STRANGE BIRDS AND KILLER WHALES

Because Ranger wasn't part of the sled dog team, Captain Scott untied him after the storm. Ranger still ate with the team and slept on deck at night, but he stayed with Jack during the day as the ship headed south toward Antarctica.

Jack kept busy and worked as hard as he'd promised. There were pumps to man and meals to prepare. There were ponies to feed and clothes to mend. And there was scientific work to be done, too. That was Jack's favorite, when he'd completed his more tiresome jobs. He loved working with the zoologists to collect samples of different sea animals and helping to preserve specimens.

The best part of all was drawing the different creatures they saw in the ocean. Wilson, the zoologist, taught Jack how to blend different colors of paint in the mixing trays to get just the right shade of gray for a dolphin or whale.

The crew member Jack had talked with at the docks back in Port Chalmers, Apsley Cherry-Garrard, loved the scientific work, too. Cherry, as the men called him, had a plan to collect eggs from emperor penguins once they reached Antarctica. The birds' only known nesting and breeding site was Cape Crozier, far over the ice. They'd have to go in late June — the heart of winter in Antarctica — to find eggs that hadn't already hatched.

"It will be a long, frigid journey," Cherry told Jack as they sifted through specimens they caught in a trawl net. "Sixty miles through the most dismal cold and wildest gales, most of it in the dark. But if we can collect the eggs, we may discover the missing link between birds and their reptile ancestors from long ago."

"That sounds amazing." Jack knew only a few men would make the journey to the penguin rookery; most would need to stay back to prepare for the longer trip to the South Pole. He so hoped he would be allowed to go, long and cold as that trip would be. "I could draw the emperor penguins and their eggs."

"Perhaps you shall," Cherry said with a wink. "You have quite a talent for sketching."

Jack couldn't wait to draw everything in Antarctica. Some of the crew members had been there on an earlier expedition that didn't reach the South Pole. Those men told stories of penguins, whales, and crab-eating seals with powerful jaws. Jack couldn't wait to see all of the animals of this cold, strange land. For now, he practiced by drawing Ranger, standing on the ship's deck in the sunshine.

About a week after the big storm, on a bright, sparkling day, Jack looked out over the railing and saw icebergs, gleaming in the sun.

"Are we close now?" he asked Cherry.

"We are," Cherry answered. "But we must reach our landing spot in the bay. Passing through this ice on the Ross Sea will be the slowest part of our voyage."

Cherry was right. Sometimes, the *Terra Nova* passed through open water between the ice floes. Sometimes, the ship crashed into the ice, splitting it into pieces, and pushed ahead. Sometimes, the men had to wait for the wind and currents to move the ice so the *Terra Nova* could go on. Jack used the long, slow days to sketch the whales that circled the ice floes.

"Look out at the light, dog," Jack told Ranger one morning as the sun came up in a rose-colored sky. The ship was working its way between two walls of ice as if it were traveling a road between them. "It's painted the ice all copper and pink. With purple shadows, too. I wonder if I could mix those colors in Wilson's paint box." He stared out at the sky and scratched Ranger behind the ears.

Ranger didn't understand what Jack was saying, but he liked the ear scratches. Still, he hoped this ship would soon arrive wherever it was going. Maybe then his job would be done and he would get to go home.

• • •

Day after day, the *Terra Nova* inched through the ice. Almost a month after they'd set sail from

Port Chalmers, the men celebrated Christmas, still on board the ship. They decorated with sledging flags, sang hymns, and feasted on mutton.

On the second of January, they spotted Antarctica's famous icy volcano, Mount Erebus. Steam rose from its snowcapped peak. They were close.

"Soon, we shall finally leave the ship, dog!" Jack told Ranger as he put out food for the ponies.

Jack talked to Ranger a lot. Back home, Luke did that, too. Ranger understood that people didn't expect him to answer. So he sat and listened and waited for ear scratches. That always seemed to be enough for Luke.

When the *Terra Nova* finally reached its landing place — a spot the men called Cape Evans — it was time to unload the cargo. First, the men unloaded the motor sledges — special vehicles designed to travel and haul goods over the ice. Then they brought the ponies off the ship. The dog handler, a man named Meares, unloaded the dogs and had them hauling supplies over the sea ice to a temporary camp for the rest of the day.

Ranger wasn't part of that dog team. He stayed with Jack and watched the activity until a funny bird walked up to him. It was black and white and waddling.

"Aark! Aark!" the bird squawked. Ranger barked at it, but it didn't fly away. It just aarked at him some more.

Ranger wasn't sure what to do. At home, he chased squirrels and birds in the yard all the time. He barked, and they ran. Then he chased them until they were way up a tree and the fun was over. But this bird didn't know how the game worked. It wobbled right up to Ranger and poked him on the nose with its beak.

Ranger jumped back and yelped. Jack laughed. "Poor dog! Don't be afraid of the little Adélie penguins. They're the friendly ones here."

Later, when Ranger went to the ship with Jack and the other dogs to fetch supplies, he saw pointy, black triangles slicing through the water. They were attached to enormous black-and-white creatures that rose to the surface and puffed water up from their backs.

"Killer whales — look!" Jack called to Ponting, a crew member who took lots of photographs. Ponting ran to the edge of the ice floe to take a picture, but the whales disappeared beneath the surface.

A second later, there was a great booming sound. The ice under Ranger's paws heaved up. He slid on the tilting ice and caught himself as it splashed down again.

"Watch out!" Ponting cried. Again and

again, the whales rose under the ice, ramming into it with their backs. Ponting jumped to safety on a larger floe. The sled dogs barked and yelped, trying to keep their footing on the tipping, slipping ice. Ranger stayed close to Jack, but then the ice lurched again.

A wave sloshed over the edge. Jack's feet slipped out from under him, and he slid toward the sea.

Ranger barked, but there was no one to help. Jack's eyes were full of terror. The whales were circling. Jack's hands slapped desperately at the ice, but there was nothing to hold.

Before Ranger could get to him, Jack slipped into the water and disappeared.

Chapter 5

ICE RESCUE!

Ranger barked and pawed the ice. But there was nothing he could do to help.

Ranger had trained for water rescues one summer, riding in the bow of a boat and sniffing for a training person who'd dived below. When Ranger caught the person's scent, he barked to alert Dad and Luke. They had a special rope in the boat, with a float on one end so it wouldn't sink when rescuers threw it into the water.

Ranger barked and looked around. There was no special rope here. Only the weathered lines attached to the ponies' reins. Ranger tried to get that rope in his teeth, but the pony spooked and skittered back over the ice.

"Hold on, Jack!" Ponting called. He pulled some rope from a sled, looped it over his shoulder, and leaped for the ice floe.

Ponting's feet slid out from under him. He landed hard on his back, and the rope went skidding toward the open water.

Just before it slipped into the sea, Ranger grabbed the end of the rope in his teeth and raced to find Jack. The boy tried to grab on to the edge of the ice floe, clawing and slipping.

Ranger pushed the scratchy rope against Jack's fingers. The boy gasped and flailed at the rope, but he missed and slipped underwater.

Ranger barked and pawed the rope into the water. When Jack's head appeared above the water, his lips were blue. His teeth chattered so violently that his whole face shook. But his eyes met Ranger's.

Jack reached, closed his hand around the rope, and pulled it to his chest.

"Hold on, son!" Ponting crawled to the edge and grabbed the rope. He drove a sharp pick into the ice and used it to steady himself as he pulled and tugged Jack out of the water.

The boy sprawled on the ice, panting and shivering. Ranger crouched close to Jack to warm him.

The whales hadn't attacked Jack in the water, but they hadn't left, either. Half a dozen still circled the ice floe, snorting and blowing. One raised itself nose first from the water, looking over the ice.

The whales' big, awful eyes made Jack's stomach twist. He couldn't stop shivering. He pushed himself up on his knees and reached out to pull the dog closer. He tried to say

"thank you" but his frozen lips wouldn't make the words. So he petted the dog's icy fur over and over, and hoped he understood.

The men wrapped Jack in blankets and helped him off the ice. Ranger walked beside Jack, all the way to the tent. That night, he squeezed in beside Jack in the sleeping bag Captain Scott had given Jack for the journey.

Jack fell asleep right away. Ranger listened to the boy's soft snores and waited for something to happen.

At home, when Ranger did search-and-rescue training, he had to find one person, or sometimes two. When his people were safe, his job was done.

Ranger had helped this Jack boy twice now — once, when he was almost swept off the ship and again today. When would he get to go home?

• • •

In the days that followed, Ranger walked beside Jack as they unloaded supplies from the *Terra Nova*. They fed the ponies each morning and listened to the sounds of hammering as the men worked to build a hut.

"A home fit for kings," Cherry declared.

"Is it big enough?" After the supplies were unloaded, some of the men took the ship to another location to get rock and soil samples from a different part of the shore. But Jack still didn't see how the twenty-five who remained were going to fit in the hut they were building.

"Certainly. It'll be fifty feet long and twenty-five feet wide," Cherry said. "And with seaweed insulation, we'll be plenty warm inside."

The men moved into their new hut on the eighteenth of January. Jack helped load supplies into the building where they would spend the winter.

Even when the hut was finished, there was much work to do. The men hunted seals and penguins and carved out ice caves to store the meat. At first, Jack hated the idea of eating such curious creatures, but then Cherry told him about scurvy.

"You go too long without fresh produce or meat, and you'll be so tired you can barely rise in the morning. You'll have aching bones and bloody gums. Then your teeth'll fall out and go clattering all over the ice."

Jack ate the fresh meat and didn't complain.

They'd been in the hut a week when Captain Scott announced it was time to lay supplies for their nine-hundred-mile journey from Cape Evans to the South Pole. They would make several trips before the big one — placing food and fuel at planned locations along the way.

Jack sighed as he worked alongside Cherry. He was tired of the boring work of getting ready. When he'd stolen aboard the ship back in Port Chalmers, he'd been imagining his grandfather's heroic journey to work in the gold mines. He'd seen himself leading a team to the pole, planting a flag in triumph — not mending trousers and frying seal livers for breakfast.

"I wish we were going to the South Pole now." Jack loaded a crate of biscuits and a box full of medicine and supplies. Ranger's first aid kit was in there, too. "This trip has been all work and no adventure."

"This isn't a game, lad." Cherry tied off a rope and turned to Jack. His voice was sharp. "Failing to prepare means more than not reaching the pole. It could well mean starving or freezing to death on the way." He gestured at the pile of fuel and supplies. "You want to finish helping me load now?"

Jack nodded and reached for a crate of pemmican. He knew Cherry was right. He'd heard stories of other Antarctic explorers — men like Cook and Ross and Shackleton, who'd struggled with blizzards and snow blindness and frostbite. It was no easy voyage.

But this trip would end with success. Jack believed it with every bit of his heart. They would reach the South Pole. They would be the first.

And he couldn't wait for the *real* journey to begin.

Chapter 6

CRACKS IN THE ICE

When the supplies were prepared, twelve men, eight ponies, two dog teams, Jack, and Ranger set out over the sea ice. It was breaking up in places, so they chose their route carefully. Finally, the ponies and dog teams pulled the sleds onto what Cherry told Jack was called the "barrier," the great ice shelf between the mountains and sea.

"The snow is softer here. The ponies are struggling," Jack said as he and Cherry walked along behind the horses. "Do we have more snowshoes for them?" The special pony snowshoes, made of wire and bamboo, seemed to help. But Jack could only find one pair.

Cherry shook his head. "The rest are back at the ship. There wasn't time for the horses to train with them. They'll be all right with some rest," Cherry added. He looked off to the left. "What's that?"

Jack squinted into the distance and saw two snowy mounds. He and the other men held the ponies while Captain Scott walked over to the mounds and brushed away the snow.

"They're tents!" Cherry said. "From the Shackleton expedition, no doubt." Three years earlier, Ernest Shackleton and his crew had explored the Beardmore Glacier and climbed Mount Erebus. They'd traveled hundreds of miles over ice and snow, but they never reached the South Pole. That victory was still to be claimed.

All day, Jack imagined what it would be like after they reached the South Pole. "Those bands and cheers at the *Terra Nova*'s departure will be nothing compared to the fanfare that greets us when we return, dog." He patted Ranger's head as they trudged on through the snow.

Ranger couldn't slow down to enjoy the petting. He'd joined one of the dog teams to help pull the sled full of supplies. He liked the work, but the lead dog, Osman, growled at him. Ranger did his best to stay out of Osman's way.

The snow was deep, and the travel was slow. Five miles one day. Ten the next. Then a blizzard kept the men in their tents for three days.

Ranger was hungry. He could tell the other animals were, too. The horses didn't have enough energy to pull the huge loads. Scott ordered men to take some of the ponies back to camp early. The rest grew thinner and thinner.

The sled dogs were getting lean, too. They were so hungry that one team attacked a pony that was stuck in a snowdrift. The horses fought off the dogs, but the pony was hurt, too weak to travel even another mile before the men made camp.

In the tent that night, Jack leaned down and gave Ranger the last of his pemmican. "It will be all right, dog." Jack's voice trembled. "Father always said that great rewards require great risk."

Ranger nuzzled Jack's hand and ate the pemmican. It tasted meaty, and that was good. But it wasn't like the roast beef Luke's mother made at home.

Ranger missed home meat. He missed playing in the snow with Luke and Sadie. He missed going inside and curling up by the fireplace. And it was starting to feel like his job here wouldn't be done for a long, long time. Ranger's first aid kit was packed on one of the sleds. Every day, as he pulled with the other dogs, he listened for the old box to hum. But it stayed quiet.

. . .

They traveled a few more days through soft and blowing snow before Scott decided it was time to head back to camp. The men built a pyramid-shaped tower of snow around a heap of supplies. They buried food, oil, and oats for the horses, and marked the pile with a flag on a bamboo pole.

The men traveled in three teams on the return trip. A few went with the ponies. Cherry, Wilson, and Jack took one dog team. Captain Scott and Meares went with the other.

Ranger and Osman were the lead dogs for

that team. It went well at first. Osman finally seemed to be accepting Ranger as part of the pack. Both dogs were strong. The two teams traveled seventy-eight miles in the first three days of the return trip.

But then Captain Scott decided to cut a corner on their planned route to save time. The shortcut was full of delays. The snow and ice were riddled with crevasses, great gaping cracks that could swallow a man in an instant.

The ice felt different under Ranger's paws here. Hollow and weak. It made the hair on his neck stand up.

The teams had to slow down. They crossed more crevasses than Jack could count. "Good job, dog!" he called over to Ranger, who was leading the other sled team beside Osman.

But at that moment, the rear dogs on that team fell into a crevasse and dropped out of sight. The two dogs in front of them scrambled and clawed at the edge of the gaping crack, but they slipped in, too.

Then another two dogs, and another.

Finally, only Osman and Ranger were left, struggling to keep a foothold. The sled had come to a stop on the other side of the crevasse.

"Whoa!" Cherry shouted. He and Jack tethered their team and ran to help.

"Easy, dogs . . . easy," Jack called to Osman and Ranger as they tried to keep their footing. The rest of the team hung in their harnesses in midair. Ranger and Osman pulled against the weight of the dogs that had fallen, but the load was too heavy. They couldn't gain even an inch.

Ranger whimpered. If he and Osman couldn't hold on, all the dogs would be lost down the crevasse. The supplies, too. The pemmican and biscuits, the medicine and tools, and Ranger's first aid kit. How would Jack and the other men survive the rest of their journey? And how would Ranger ever get home?

Ranger crouched low. He pulled against the rope with all his might.

But his paws were slipping. He knew he couldn't last much longer.

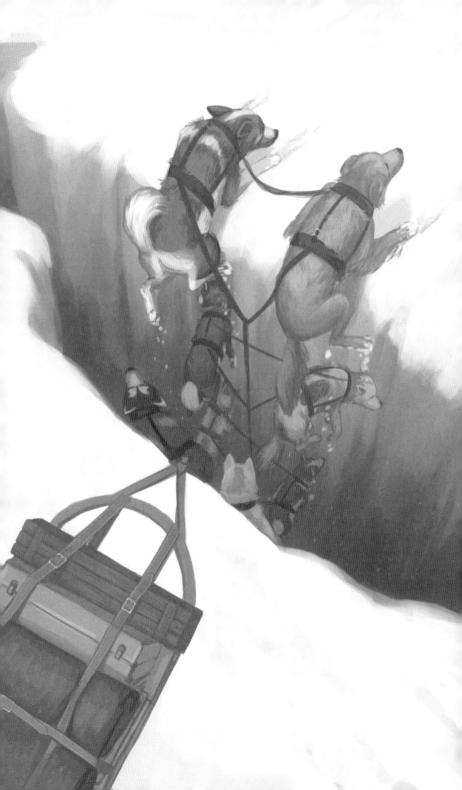

Chapter 7

SAVE THE SLED!

"Save the sled!" someone shouted. Jack helped Cherry and Wilson pull it from the edge of the crevasse. They drove a peg into the ice and tethered the sled so it wouldn't fall in, too.

"What about the dogs?" Jack called. Ranger and Osman strained under the weight of the rest of the team. The other dogs dangled in midair, howling as the lines cut into their fur. Two had already slipped from their harnesses. They'd landed on a snow ledge that must have been sixty or seventy feet down. Jack could hear them yelping and whimpering below.

"We'll haul them up. Ready? Pull!" Captain Scott and Meares heaved on the rope while Jack and Cherry held the sled so it wouldn't slip.

Scott and Meares grunted and strained, but the rope that connected Ranger and Osman to the rest of the team was pulled tight by the dogs' weight. It cut into the snow at the edge of the crevasse. The men couldn't move it to lift the rest of the team.

Jack peered into the crevasse. "They're fighting down there!" The dangling dogs barked and snapped at one another as they tried hopelessly to get a foothold on the edge of the crevasse. "We have to do something!"

Ranger let out a choked whimper as he slipped toward the crevasse. The harness was tightening around his chest and neck.

"Hold on, dog!" Jack shouted.

Finally, Captain Scott and the other men managed to get some slack on the line. Ranger felt the pull on his neck and shoulders ease. Then Jack was there beside him, cutting him and Osman free from their harnesses.

"You did such a good job," Jack told Ranger, petting his head and back. Ranger winced. His neck was sore from where the harness had cut into his fur. But he'd held on long enough to save the rest of the team. The men had hold of them now and wouldn't let them fall.

"Good job, dog!" Jack said again. And Ranger waited. He tipped his ear toward the sled. He listened for his first aid kit to hum the way it did when his job was finished and it was time to go home. But the only sounds coming from the sled were the voices of men, getting ready to pull up the rest of the dog team.

"Ready? Pull!" The men hauled together. They brought up one dog. Then they moved the sled and used it as a bridge over the crevasse to pull up the rest. Two by two, they lifted the battered dogs into the sled and cut them from their harnesses.

"That's the last of them," Cherry said, rubbing his fur mitts together to brush off the snow.

"No." Jack shook his head. There were still two dogs stranded on the snow ledge. He pointed into the crevasse. "We can't leave them."

One of the men shook his head. "We must," he said. "It is far too dangerous to —"

"The boy is right," Captain Scott interrupted. "I will go down to fetch them. The rope is long enough." The captain tied a knot in the alpine rope so the others could lower him down. Little by little, they eased him into the icy dark.

Jack peered over the edge of the crevasse. When Scott reached the snow ledge, he retied the line so the men could lift the dogs to safety. Then they brought Scott back up, too.

The wind was howling, so the men pitched a tent for some shelter. They ate some pemmican and biscuits and mended the dog harnesses. Then they set out again.

"Sixteen miles for the day," Cherry said as they set up camp to sleep later on. "Not bad given that we almost ended the whole journey in a crevasse."

Jack squeezed his sleeping bag around him. The golden dog curled up beside him. Jack was glad no one suggested that the dog sleep outside tonight. His dog and Osman had saved the sled today. The dogs had saved all of them.

Jack's fingers burned from frostbite, but inside, he felt strangely warm. He'd proven himself on this trip to lay the supplies. No one looked at him as the boy stowaway anymore.

He was a member of the crew. When they finally made their voyage to the South Pole, he knew he'd be one of the heroes in the photograph. It would be in the newspaper back home, with the flag flying over the ice. And Jack Nin smiling proudly beside it.

Chapter 8

STRANDED AT SEA

But sad news greeted the men when they arrived at camp the next day. Of the three ponies that had set out to return from laying supplies, only one had survived. Captain Scott took the news hard. Jack wondered if that was because he loved horses, or because he knew that it meant there was more trouble ahead.

And there was even worse news in a letter that had arrived from the ship. Roald Amundsen, the Norwegian explorer who was also hoping to claim the South Pole, was already set up with his dog teams at the Bay of Whales, ready to begin his trip over land.

Captain Scott's hands shook as he held the letter. "How did he get so many dogs safely onto the ice? This is . . . this is . . ."

"A disaster, is what it is," Cherry whispered to Jack.

The captain took a deep breath. "We shall proceed as planned. As if this never happened." But his lips were pressed together, and his face was flushed.

"Can't we still get there first? We'll have to be quicker is all," Jack said.

Cherry sighed. "We shall try, my friend. But Amundsen's position at the Bay of Whales makes his journey some sixty miles shorter than ours. And he has dogs."

"We have dogs," Jack said, petting Ranger on the head.

Cherry smiled, but his mouth was a tight line across his face. "Not enough. We have ponies — what's left of them — and they aren't handling the terrain nearly as well."

• • •

Soon, it was time to lay more supplies. Jack whistled in the hut as he pulled on his boots. His skin was chafed and rough now. He was getting used to the cold and wind. He worked hard and never complained. He felt sure Captain Scott would choose him for the team that would make the final push to the South Pole.

"And we shall get there first," Jack told Ranger as they prepared to head out onto the barrier again.

They pulled sleds out to the depot they called Corner Camp. There, they unloaded food, oil, and gear. When they left, Jack looked back at the flag that marked their cache. He imagined the day he'd be back in this place, making use of the oil and eating biscuits on his *real* journey, to the South Pole.

But more supplies had to be packed and transported out onto the snow and ice before that final trip could happen. Mile after snowy mile, Ranger walked beside Jack or helped Osman pull the sled. Mile after mile, he wondered when this trip would end.

One night in early March while the team was returning from a supply run, Ranger was curled up beside Jack's sleeping bag in the tent, dreaming of home and summer. There were squirrels and a barbecue in his dream. Someone had just dropped a hot dog under the picnic table when Ranger woke up to a man shouting.

"It's breaking up!" A man named Bowers flung open the tent and shouted, "Pack up the supplies! The ice is breaking up!"

Jack scrambled out of his sleeping bag and stumbled outside in his socks. Nothing could have prepared him for what he saw.

When they'd ended their march for the day and made camp, it had been on safe, solid ice, far from the open water. But as they slept, that ice had broken apart. Now Jack, Ranger, and the rest of the team floated on a slab no more than thirty yards long. It had broken underneath the line that secured their sleds. One of the ponies was gone, a hungry, dark tongue of water where the ice had split beneath it. The sleds were still tied up, on the next floe. They'd been dragged all the way to the edge of the ice.

"Help me save the supplies!" Bowers ran to

a place where the two ice floes were touching. Cherry and Jack helped him drag the heavy sleds across. Now all the men and supplies were crowded on the same chunk of ice.

Jack shivered in the frigid dark. The waves churned like an angry cauldron. Killer whales kept popping their heads up to see over the edge of the floe.

"Hurry! We have to move!" Bowers shouted. The men packed up their supplies and tents. They harnessed the ponies while the ice heaved under their feet. "Our only hope is to jump from ice floe to ice floe until we get to stable ground!"

"Go on, Nobby! Haw!" Cherry's pony jumped from the edge of their ice floe onto another one. The others followed. Jack helped bring the sleds to the next slab of ice.

"Ready, dog?" Jack swallowed hard. The ice dipped. Waves splashed up at its edge. What if he slipped into the water with all those black fins circling?

Ranger nudged Jack's mitt and barked.

"Me first? Is that it, dog?" Jack took a deep breath and jumped. His feet slid when he landed.

Cherry grabbed his arm to steady him. "All right, son?"

Jack nodded and turned to Ranger. "Come on, dog!"

Ranger jumped and skidded into Jack on the other ice floe.

Once all the animals and men and supplies were together, they waited for another ice floe to drift close. When it bumped against them, the men jumped the ponies over the gap. Then they followed with the sleds.

Jump.

Everyone together.

Wait . . .

Wait . . .

Bump.

Jump again.

Jack's heart pounded with every swell of the waves. He knew the wind could shift at any second and whisk them all out to sea. The other men must have understood that, too, but they worked and talked as if this were just another day. During an especially long wait, Cherry even brought out biscuits and chocolate and passed them around.

After six hours of jumping from ice floe to ice floe, they finally got close to the stable ice of the barrier.

"We're saved!" shouted Cherry. He raced across the last big ice floe.

Jack followed. He'd never been more ready to feel solid ground under his boots.

But when they ran up the slope of that last slab of ice, all Jack's hopes fell from under

him. There must have been at least thirty feet of water between the ice where he stood and the safety of the barrier.

Thirty feet of wild, angry sea. The water churned with smashed-up ice and circling killer whales.

Jack looked at Cherry. "How will we —"

Then the ice cracked. It tipped, and Jack slid back toward the supplies. He clung to a sled and looked around.

There was no safe path to the barrier. They were stuck. And their ice floe had split in two.

Chapter 9

TRACKING CAPTAIN SCOTT

The men huddled on the half slab of ice that remained and talked about what to do. There was no way to get across that huge span of water. Not here. Not with all the ponies and supplies.

"We must reach Captain Scott," Cherry said. "If one of us goes alone, he'll be able to find a floe that's touching the barrier. Then he can cross and go to camp to bring help."

The man named Crean volunteered to go. He stuffed his pockets with food and turned to the others. "I'll be back soon. With help."

Ranger felt a strange tug to follow. He thought about his search-and-rescue training with Luke and Dad. Sometimes, when you found a person who was in trouble, you stayed and barked until help arrived. But this time, help was far away. Ranger's barks would never be heard over the waves. In times like this, you had to go get help and bring it back.

Ranger barked and raced to Crean's side.

"Go on, dog," the man said. "Stay and wait with the rest of them."

Jack ran to Ranger. He knelt down and looked into the dog's brown eyes. Then he looked up at Crean. "He's a good dog. And smart. You should take him in case you need help finding the way back."

"All right then," Crean said, slapping his thigh. Ranger trotted up to him. "You ready to jump?"

Ranger followed Crean to the edge of the ice floe. They waited for another piece of ice to drift closer. Then they jumped — and they were off.

• • •

Jack and the other men stayed with the ponies. They ate biscuits and talked about their families to pass the time.

Cherry's father was a British army officer who'd seen many adventures in his day.

Bowers had lost his father when he was young. His mother had raised him and his sisters.

"My father died just over a year ago. He was a market gardener," Jack said. "My grandfather . . ." He stood up a little taller. "My grandfather left his home in China to mine for gold in New Zealand so he could help his family. That's what I'm doing, too."

"You're mining gold? Hadn't heard there was treasure on the ice," Bowers said with a laugh.

Jack's face burned, even in the cold. "That's not what I meant. It's . . . it's a different sort of treasure on this trip," he said.

"Indeed," Cherry said quietly. "I only hope we survive to reach it."

• • •

Five ice floes away, Ranger stood with Crean, waiting for another slab to blow close enough to jump. Ranger's paws hurt. Balls of ice had gotten stuck in the fur between his toes. Every time he landed, they dug into his skin.

"Ready, dog?" Crean crouched and leaped onto another floe, and Ranger followed.

Again and again they jumped. The water was full of penguins and seals and killer whales. Ranger ignored them all and did his work. He jumped and waited and jumped and waited until, finally, they reached an ice floe that was touching the barrier. But the solid ice was up high — higher than Crean or Ranger could jump.

"We'll not give up now, dog." Crean put a harness on Ranger and tied one end of the rope to his belt. He used his ski stick to dig a hole in the side of the barrier ice, to use as a step. He straddled the water with one foot on that step and the other way down on the shifting, bobbing ice floe.

Ranger whined. It didn't look safe. He wasn't sure what he'd do if this man fell into the sea. They were attached to each other by that rope. The man was big. Ranger would be pulled in with him. And there was no one here to bark at for help.

Crean stuck his ski stick into the top of the barrier ice and used it to spring himself up. He flung his leg over the edge and climbed onto the barrier. Then he grabbed the rope between his fur mitts. "Ready, dog?"

Ranger felt the harness tighten around his chest. Then his paws lifted off the ice, and the man pulled him up onto the snow beside him. "Now," Crean said, "let's find the captain."

It wasn't long before Ranger picked up the scent of the men who'd been traveling back and forth, laying supplies. He barked and led Crean to the camp. One of the men must have seen them coming; he rushed out on skis to meet them and brought them to Captain Scott.

The captain and another crewmember named Oates gathered up some supplies. Then Ranger set out to lead them back to the ice.

• • •

Jack had almost given up hope. Every time he thought he saw Crean coming back with help, it turned out to be a group of emperor penguins. It was strange how much they looked like men from a distance.

But finally, Jack heard a bark. When he looked up, he saw not only Ranger but Crean and Scott and Oates — who were definitely not penguins. They were saved!

"Use the sled as a ladder and climb up onto the barrier!" Captain Scott shouted.

"What about the supplies?" Bowers called.

"I don't care a bit about the ponies and the sleds!" the captain hollered down. "It's you I want, and I am going to see you safe up here on the barrier before I do anything else."

And so they climbed up. Jack was thankful to be standing on ice that wasn't lurching and heaving beneath him.

"My dear chaps," Captain Scott said after

the last man reached the top. "You can't think how glad I am to see you safe."

Jack thought he could guess. He was pretty glad to see the captain, too. He was even happier to see his dog. He wasn't the dog's real owner, of course. But he'd come to think of the shaggy golden hound as his. He hoped the dog felt the same way.

Captain Scott let them try to recover some of their supplies. In the end, they saved everything except two ponies that fell into the sea. It was sad, and Jack couldn't help thinking of his own horse, Whetu. But he knew the day could have ended so much worse.

That night, they camped far from the edge of the open water. Still, Jack checked outside every so often to make sure the ice wasn't breaking up.

When Jack finally settled to sleep, Ranger lay awake in the stuffy tent. He'd worked hard again today. He'd jumped across all those rivers in the ice. He'd gone to get the captain. He'd brought help, and now everyone was safe.

When would he get to go home?

Chapter 10

DAYS OF DARKNESS

The journey to reach the South Pole couldn't happen until late October, when spring truly arrived in Antarctica. But the men had other jobs for the dark winter months of May and June. They mended clothes and prepared supplies. Cherry got ready for his journey to Cape Crozier to collect eggs from the emperor penguins for scientists to study back home.

"Wouldn't this journey be easier with more daylight?" Jack asked as they measured pemmican rations for the trip. There was no sunrise in Antarctica in the darkest winter months — only twilight and dark.

"It'll be too late to collect eggs then," Cherry said. "By September, the chicks will have hatched."

So it was June 27, one of the darkest days of the year, when Cherry, Bowers, Wilson, and Jack set out pulling two sleds, one behind the other. They brought supplies and food for the five-week journey — pemmican, biscuits, butter, and tea, along with horse meat for Ranger. Jack convinced the men to bring him along, since he'd managed to lead Captain Scott to the spot where Jack and the others had been stranded when the ice broke up.

Right away, Jack realized this trip would be different. When even the middle of the day was dark, the cold felt colder. The gales seemed to blow stronger. Jack's sweat froze on his

clothes and turned them stiff as boards. His breath froze on his balaclava.

The days were endless frozen marches. The nights seemed to last forever. It was never truly warm enough for Jack to sleep, even with Ranger squeezed into the bag beside him. His teeth chattered. Sometimes, his whole body shook uncontrollably with the cold. There was nothing he could do but hold on to the dog and wait for it to stop.

The temperature was forty-seven degrees below zero the day Jack took off his fur mitts so he could get a better grip on the ropes to haul the sled. The cold wind stung his hands in an instant. Every finger was frostbitten and covered in blisters by the time Jack forced his way into his frozen sleeping bag that night.

Usually, Ranger liked winter. His coat was thick, and for seven months, he'd been eating lots of meat and fat, like the other sled dogs.

Still, he had never been this cold. He'd done some of his search-and-rescue training in the snowy mountains with Luke and Dad, but that had been different. Ranger had been practicing to find people who were trapped in avalanches and buried in snow. It had been daytime, and warmer, and it hadn't gone on forever like this.

During that avalanche training, Ranger had sat beside Dad on a special chair that climbed the mountain. When they got to the top, he'd run down the snowy slope on a leash while Dad skied slowly back and forth over the trail. Ranger had to sniff the cold air to find the scent of a person who was buried in the snow. When he found the person, he dug and barked until rescue people with shovels came to help.

Then the person climbed out of the snow, and Ranger went home with Luke and Dad.

Home.

Ranger dreamed of his home family all night. In the morning, he nosed his way out of Jack's icy sleeping bag and wondered if this dark, cold trip would ever end.

It took the men nineteen days to reach Cape Crozier. They set to work building an igloo for shelter from the wind. The men piled up rock walls and banked them with snow. They used one of the sleds as a beam and a big sheet of green canvas for the roof.

When the men finally found the emperor penguins, the birds squawked and trumpeted wildly. Their calls echoed off the cliffs over the sea ice.

Jack stayed back with Ranger while the others went to collect eggs. He felt torn, watching the penguins shuffle along, trying not to lose the eggs on top of their feet.

Jack wanted the scientific mission to be a success. He couldn't imagine coming all this way for nothing. But at the same time, he felt sad for the penguins, having their eggs taken from them, when they'd worked so hard to keep them warm.

When the men headed back to their igloo, they carried three birds they'd killed for blubber to use in their stove, and five eggs. Two of the eggs broke in Cherry's mitts on the way back. They hoped to preserve the other three.

Jack imagined the welcome that would greet them when the *Terra Nova* returned to New Zealand. They'd bring not just penguin eggs but stories of the South Pole, a place no man had ever seen before.

Jack's mother and his brothers would be there, all cheering for him. He'd have such amazing things to show them, so many stories to tell. And he'd arrive with money for his family, just like his grandfather had when he'd come home from the gold mines.

By the time the men returned to camp, another blizzard was blowing over the snow. Snow whipped into the igloo in a hundred places and drifted over their sleeping bags while they slept.

In the morning, the wind kept howling. Jack gathered every bit of loose snow he could find and packed it into the cracks. The other men cut huge squares of snow to help hold down the roof. They set up the tent beside the igloo and moved much of their gear inside it. They lit the blubber stove and warmed themselves in the heat it gave off before they worked their way back into frozen sleeping bags for the night.

"Things must improve," said Wilson.

His voice was calm, as it always was, even in the worst weather. Jack settled into his stiff, frozen sleeping bag, thankful for that. He drifted to sleep.

But it wasn't long before he woke to wind, howling and shrieking louder than before.

Then Bowers shouted, "The tent has gone!"

Chapter 11

BLIZZARD!

Jack struggled out of his frozen sleeping bag to the igloo door. Cherry and Bowers pushed it open. They fought their way against the wind to where the tent had been and rushed to save the supplies left behind. It was a wonder the supplies hadn't blown away, too, but nothing was missing except two pieces of the cooker. The men battled the wind to save their gear. Walls of snow pushed them back, but piece by piece, they passed their supplies inside the igloo.

The wind was wild. It was moving the huge blocks of snow the men had put on the roof to hold it down. What would they do if the roof blew off? Where would they go?

Nowhere, Jack thought. There was nowhere they could take shelter. He looked up at Cherry. "What if the igloo goes, too?"

"With walls of rock? That isn't likely," Cherry said, but his voice trembled.

It wasn't long before the blocks of snow slid off the roof in the wind. The canvas cover slammed up and down, as if some great monster had hold of the cloth in its fist.

The men tried to keep up their routine. They heated some pemmican on their stove and ate. When they were full, they set to work, plugging gaps in the igloo with socks and mitts. But the snow kept drifting in.

"Listen to me!" Wilson bellowed over the wind, pulling Jack close. "If the roof goes, our only hope is to shelter in our bags. Roll over so you're covering the opening and get yourself

drifted in. After that, all we can do is wait for the blizzard to pass."

The rocks of the walls were lifting up, shaking, while the roof crashed up and down.

Cherry said something, but no one could hear him over the wind.

"The ropes!" he called. "Lash the alpine rope over the roof outside to hold it down!"

"Impossible!" Bowers shouted.

And then the roof went. In an instant, the green canvas split into shreds, flapping and thundering in the wind.

"Watch out!" Cherry roared as the highest rocks of the igloo walls caved in on them.

Jack dived for his sleeping bag and wiggled his way inside through the ice. "Come on, dog!" He held open a space for Ranger to crawl in beside him.

Jack pulled Ranger close. He petted the

dog's stiff, frozen fur, and shivered while the wind howled.

It was the longest night of Jack's life, and the darkness pressed in on his heart. How could they get back without a tent for shelter on the return trip?

Jack moved his feet and hands inside his bag as best he could, trying to stay warm. Cherry and Bowers sang in their sleeping bags — all the songs they knew, it seemed to Jack. The men didn't have sweet voices, like his mother, and they weren't singing Maori lullabies. But their voices calmed Jack's racing heart a little.

He tried to rest as the snow drifted in. Every once in a while, he hunched up his body and tried to shake off the snow. He figured out that if he opened the flaps of his bag just a bit, he could reach out and get pinches of snow to bring in. Jack put a bit of snow in his mouth and waited for it to melt to water. He scraped off some more snow, and Ranger lapped it up. At least they wouldn't be thirsty.

Finally, after two more days, the blizzard began to fade.

Cherry was the first out of his sleeping bag. "We have to find the tent," he said.

"We're nine hundred feet up a mountain with the wind blowing out to sea," Bowers said. "The tent could be halfway to New Zealand by now."

Just the mention of home made Jack's heart ache. Everything ached. His shoulder, from where the harness cut into him. His frozen fingers. His empty stomach. They hadn't eaten in two days.

Jack wanted to be back at camp, with a full meal instead of pemmican and tea. But camp was seventy miles away. And there was no way to get there without a tent.

So Jack set out with Cherry and Wilson to search. They were about to explore a ridge when they heard Bowers shout from the bottom of a steep slope. He'd found the tent!

Two poles were broken, but the tent itself was fine. So the men brought it back and set it up for the night.

When they started toward camp, a cold, miserable wind was blowing over the ice. Each day felt longer than the last.

Jack counted them down, hoping his guesses were right, hoping there would be no blizzards to slow them down.

"Six more days, dog," he told Ranger as they trudged through the snow.

"Five more days!" he said the next day, as they pulled Bowers out of a crevasse.

They made good progress, so then there were four more days. Then three, and two, and one.

On the last day, the men pulled their sled up to the hut. They stood outside, trying to get out of their frozen harnesses.

Finally, the door opened. "Good God! Here is the Crozier party!" someone said.

They had done it. Survived a five-week journey over snow and ice, in the darkness of the polar winter. They'd come back exhausted, with withered hands and frostbitten fingers. But they'd done it.

Jack dropped to his knees to hug Ranger after they stepped into the hut. Warmth had never felt so wonderful. "We made it home, dog."

Home.

Ranger leaned into Jack's hug. He was glad for the warmth.

But this was a long way from home.

Chapter 12

RACE TO THE SOUTH POLE

Finally, the days grew lighter. The men sang as they worked, getting ready for their trip to the South Pole. They stopped to pat Ranger's head and slipped him bits of pemmican.

Ranger was getting used to this strange, fatty meat. It didn't taste as good as the hamburger pieces Luke dropped him under the picnic table at home, but it was meat. And any meat was better than no meat at all.

• • •

When the polar party set out from Cape Evans, Ranger was with Osman, pulling one of the sleds. The dogs were better on ice than the ponies that kept slipping and sinking into the snow.

"Will the ponies be all right?" Jack asked Cherry one night.

Cherry shook his head. "They're not suited for this kind of travel, and they are suffering. Captain Scott only intends to take them a bit farther," he said. "Then he'll shoot them and leave the meat behind for the dogs to eat on the return trip."

"He's going to kill them? He can't do that! It's not right. It's —"

"Survival," Cherry said quietly. "There isn't enough food. We need the meat for the dogs. And the ponies aren't going to make it anyway."

So the dogs pulled some of the sleds, and the men, strapped into harnesses, hauled the rest on skis. Some days, they made only eight or ten miles before another blizzard chased them into their tents.

One morning, Jack couldn't find his goggles. Had he lost them in the snow? There was no time to look; they had to start out again.

All day, the sun glistened on the icy surface of the Beardmore Glacier. Jack felt as if his eyes were filled with scratchy sand that tears wouldn't wash away. Soon, they were so swollen he could barely see the tips of his skis. Ranger stayed close by Jack's side and nudged him if he started drifting toward the edge of a crevasse.

When they stopped for the day, Cherry gave Jack tea leaves tied into cotton to press against his eyes. It soothed them a little. But it didn't soothe the scratchy feeling that had been growing all day in Jack's heart.

He'd overheard Captain Scott talking, fretting over the rations. They'd planned their laying of supplies carefully so they'd have food for the entire trip to the South Pole and return. But now they were already eating food that should have been saved for the last stages of the journey. What would they eat later on?

Jack's pemmican and biscuits stuck in his throat that night. His eyes were still swollen shut, but he couldn't stop seeing images in his mind — so many miles of whiteness. So little food for the rest of the trip. But they had to reach the South Pole. They couldn't give up now.

Jack was about to climb into his sleeping bag when Captain Scott stepped into their tent.

"I'm afraid I have rather a blow for you," he said.

"We're going back." Jack couldn't see Cherry's face, but he heard the disappointment in his voice.

"I've thought long about this," Captain Scott said. "Our rations are slim. The two of you are weak from your winter journey to Cape Crozier." Jack felt Captain Scott's hand on his shoulder. "I'm sending you back to the base camp at Cape Evans, along with Atch, Keohane, and Silas, to wait for our return. You'll depart tomorrow."

"No!" Jack blurted. He hadn't come all this way, left his family and everything he'd ever known, to turn back. "I won't go back. I can't."

"You must," Captain Scott said. And with that, he left the tent.

Jack's eyes burned with tears. One slipped down his sunburned cheek. Jack pressed his hands into his eyes so the other men wouldn't see.

That evening, Cherry gave away his extra gear. He passed his finnesko on to Bowers, his pajama trousers to Wilson, his socks to Crean. Then he climbed into his sleeping bag with a sigh.

Jack didn't understand how Cherry could let it go so easily. How could he come so far and not fight to stay? It was wrong. Maybe Cherry accepted Captain Scott's decision, but Jack didn't.

The next day Captain Scott and his remaining team set out to the south.

Jack and Cherry and the rest of the returning party packed up their tent and started back toward Cape Evans.

The journey over the Beardmore Glacier had been long and full of trouble the first time they'd made it. But that trip had been for a good reason. They'd been on their way to a place no man had stood before.

Today, the trip over the glacier was every bit as dreary and exhausting. But this time, Jack was making it as a failure — someone Captain Scott didn't believe was strong enough or smart enough. He wasn't *enough* of anything to push on to the end.

Jack was exhausted. His muscles ached. He was sunburned and frostbitten and sick to his stomach. All he could do was keep marching over the ice, away from where he wanted to be.

A few miles into the trip, a snowy crust gave way beneath Jack's feet. He plunged into a crevasse, falling past its icy walls until the harness jerked at his middle and caught him.

Ranger barked up above.

"You all right there?" Cherry called down.

Jack didn't answer. He wasn't all right. He was so broken, he half wished the harness would just let him go. Then he wouldn't have to walk any more miles away from his dream.

But the harness held strong. Cherry and the other men pulled him up.

Later, as Jack listened to the men breathing and snoring in their frozen sleeping bags, he made a decision.

He wasn't taking one more step toward Cape Evans. He'd take a pack with some food and follow the sled tracks backward, until he found Captain Scott and the polar team. As just one man on skis, with no sled to pull, he'd catch up to them in a day — maybe less. He would sneak himself back to the team. It was no different from stowing away on the *Terra Nova* in Port Chalmers, really. And then, Captain Scott would have no choice but to let him continue on to the South Pole.

Jack eased himself out of his sleeping bag so he wouldn't wake the others. He slipped two rations of pemmican and biscuits into a carrying pack. He pulled on his fur boots and balaclava and headed for the tent door.

Jack looked back at the shaggy golden dog curled up near Cherry's sleeping bag. He thought about calling to him in a whisper. But if Jack woke the other men, his plan would be ruined. And tonight was his only chance to rejoin the polar party. Jack had to run for his dream while it was still close enough.

As quietly as he could, he stepped out of the tent.

The sky was clear, the snow bright as day. The sun never set here in December.

Jack strapped on his skis. He found yesterday's sled trail leading back over the glacier and started off across the ice to find Captain Scott.

Then, they would trek on together to the South Pole.

Chapter 13

NO TURNING BACK

The first hours were good ones. Jack listened to the swish and crunch of his skis over the crusty snow. He followed the sled tracks over ridges, up and down the waves of the glacier.

But the wind picked up. It stung Jack's eyes through the holes in his balaclava. And it did something worse.

It had snowed recently on this part of the glacier. With every push of his skis, Jack saw the sled tracks from the day before grow fainter and fainter, until he couldn't see them at all.

Jack turned to look behind him. It felt good to have the wind out of his face for a moment, but his relief didn't last. The tracks behind him were gone, too.

Jack swallowed hard. He could turn back — that would probably be best — but how would he find Cherry and the others without his tracks?

At the very least, if he used his compass and kept pushing south, he'd be going in the same direction as Captain Scott. How far could he be by now? Soon, Jack figured he'd come upon their campsite from the day before. The wind couldn't have wiped away every sign of it. It would be there. And not far past it would be Captain Scott.

Jack tried to convince himself of that as he pressed on. But the wind was telling other stories — whistling and howling. The glacier was no place to be alone.

. . .

Ranger was dreaming of bacon when Cherry rolled over onto his paw.

Ranger yelped awake.

"Sorry there, fella," Cherry said as he wiggled out of his icy sleeping bag to begin the day.

Ranger rested his nose on his paws and tried to go back to sleep. He loved bacon. The home bacon that Luke's dad cooked with waffles on Sunday mornings. In his dream, it had been sizzling in the frying pan. Luke and Sadie were in the kitchen with him, slipping him pieces under the table the way Jack gave him tastes of pemmican sometimes. Ranger liked Jack a lot, but he missed Luke. And bacon was so much better than pemmican.

Ranger gave up on sleeping and looked around the tent.

Where was Jack? The boy's sleeping bag was still here, all frozen up and stiff like he got out of it a long time ago. Ranger sniffed the bag. It still smelled like Jack. He sniffed it again and barked.

"What is it, dog?" Cherry looked over from the corner where he was trying to light their tiny portable stove. Then he looked past Ranger, to Jack's empty sleeping bag. "Where'd your boy go? Outside to relieve himself?" He frowned, walked to the tent door, and looked outside. Then he called back to the other men, "Anybody hear Jack get up this morning?"

They hadn't.

Cherry sighed. "He's just brave enough and just fool enough to have gone out looking for Scott."

Cherry put on his outer trousers and jacket, his boots and balaclava and fur mitts. He turned to Ranger. "Come on, dog. Let's go look for him."

• • •

Jack kept on going. He skied up and down the waves of the glacier. He tried to travel in a straight line, but it was impossible. The sled tracks were long gone, even though it wasn't as snowy here. He wondered how far off course he was.

Jack wanted to take a rest, to eat something and check on the compass reading, but he was afraid that even the shortest break would let Captain Scott get farther away. And he had to catch up. Soon. The food and water on his back wouldn't last more than the day. If he didn't find Scott soon, he wouldn't have shelter, either.

Jack skied faster, as if he could outrun his thoughts. But there was no getting away from the cold reality of his decision. If he didn't find Scott quickly, he would die out here on the glacier. He wouldn't go home a hero. He wouldn't go home at all. His mother and brothers would never get the help he set out to give them.

Today, out on the ice, the idea of going home without reaching the South Pole didn't seem like the worst thing in the world. It seemed like Jack's best hope. But the farther he skied, the more that hope faded.

The sun moved across the sky, and Jack skied on. There was no sign of sled tracks, no sign of Scott, nothing but ice and snow.

Jack knew he couldn't afford to stop. Not even for a few minutes. But he had to know if he was still going the right way.

Jack held his poles in one hand and used his teeth to pull off his other mitt. He ignored the icy burn of the wind, reached behind his pack to unbuckle it, and fumbled with frozen fingers until he found the compass.

Then his right foot broke through a crust of snow. In a heartbeat, Jack found himself clinging to the edge of a crevasse. His one mitt slipped as he tried to hold on. With his other hand, red and raw and exposed, Jack clawed at the ice, trying to pull himself up. His ski dangled and flailed over the icy darkness below.

Every time he tried to pull himself up, the crumbling snow gave way. Jack slipped closer and closer to the edge. His fingers on his exposed hand were scratched and bleeding, but he couldn't feel them anymore. He could only watch as they slipped closer and closer to the edge.

Jack knew he couldn't hold on forever. He summoned all his strength and tried to heave himself up. He was almost there when the edge of the ice broke off.

Jack's stomach rose into his throat. The ice walls rushed past as he fell. One of his skis caught in the ice. Jack's leg twisted, and his knee gave a sickening pop. Then the ski was gone, and he was falling again.

Just when it felt like he might plunge into the darkness forever, Jack thumped on his back onto a snow shelf. He landed so hard he couldn't breathe.

Finally, he sucked in a great gasp of air and then another. Jack's knee throbbed with pain. His heart pounded in his chest as he lay on the hard-packed snow.

How far had he fallen? Jack was afraid to look. He was afraid to move. He knew he was lucky to be alive. The snow shelf had saved him.

But then, Jack looked up. The light of the polar sky was far, far above him. The icy walls of the crevasse were smooth and slippery, with nothing that even resembled a foothold. He was trapped.

The snow shelf hadn't saved his life. It might only have delayed his death.

Chapter 14

Dog Kisses and Dreams

Ranger led Cherry over the glacier. Jack's ski tracks disappeared after a little while, but the wind hadn't wiped out his scent. And Jack's smell was the only one over this long, lonely stretch of ice and snow.

Ranger followed the boy's scent up and down the snowy waves. The wind blew, and Cherry hurried Ranger along.

"Come on, dog! He won't last long in this weather."

Ranger tracked Jack as quickly as he could. But sometimes, he lost the scent and had to circle to find it again. Sometimes, his paws made a hollow sound on the snowy ice, because it was only a thin crust with cold, open space below.

Ranger was crossing a stretch of that kind of ice when Cherry shouted behind him.

"Whoa!"

When Ranger turned around, Cherry was gone. He'd broken through the crust of snow and fallen into a crevasse. Carefully, Ranger crept to the edge.

This crevasse wasn't deep. The man wasn't hurt. But he couldn't get out. And he was too big for Ranger to help, even with a rope.

Cherry stood at the bottom of the crack, shaking his head. "What was I thinking, coming alone?" he said to himself, and slammed one of his mitts against the icy wall of the crevasse.

Ranger barked.

Cherry looked up. He sighed. "Think you can find the camp again, dog?"

Find?

Find!

Ranger pawed at the snow and barked again. The Cherry man needed help. But Ranger couldn't find Jack now. Cherry needed someone bigger than Jack or Ranger to get him out of the snowy hole.

"Get help! Go on! Go to the camp and bring help!" Cherry shouted up at Ranger.

Ranger turned and started back. He wanted to run, but he didn't trust this strange-sounding snow that broke under men's feet. Carefully, as quickly as he could without losing the scent or falling into one of the hungry snow holes, he tracked his way back to camp.

When he got there, he barked at the door of the tent until one of the men came outside. "Oh no," the man said.

Ranger pawed at the snow and took a few steps toward the place where Cherry was stuck. He barked again.

The man looked at Ranger. Then he called into the tent. "The dog's come back alone, barking up a storm! I think Cherry's in trouble. Get the alpine rope and some provisions, and we'll see where he takes us."

It wasn't long before the men were bundled in their furs and balaclavas. They harnessed themselves to a sled full of supplies and equipment, and Ranger led them over the ice and snow.

The first miles were quiet. But with every step, Cherry's scent grew stronger. Finally, Ranger barked.

Cherry's voice answered from down in the ice. "I'm here! Hello! Here!"

The other men used the alpine rope to pull him back up onto the glacier. "I never should have gone out on my own with the dog," Cherry said, untying the rope. "I thought I might catch up with young Jack, but . . ." Cherry shook his head. "We have to continue on, back to Cape Evans." Cherry and the other men started back toward the camp.

No! Ranger barked. He could still pick up Jack's scent in the air. Jack wasn't here, but he wasn't far.

Ranger barked again. When he'd done his search-and-rescue training with Luke and Dad, there were times when more than one person needed help. Ranger would find the first person and lead rescuers to him or her. Then, the trainers would say, "Find more!" and Ranger would keep smelling, keep searching, until he found everyone who needed help.

Where were the men going? They needed to find *more*!

Ranger barked and barked. He raced in

front of the men and barked some more. Then he ran back out, toward the scent trail he wanted to follow.

Finally, Cherry looked at the other men. "Let's see where he goes. Not far," he said. "We can't go far. But . . ." He looked at Ranger and nodded his head. "This dog loves that boy. He wants us to follow him. Maybe he knows something we don't."

• • •

Jack couldn't tell how much time had gone by since he fell into the crevasse. The all-night polar sun didn't offer much help when it came to measuring hours. But he knew that the minutes were passing. Every one made it less likely he'd ever go home.

Home.

Jack had been so hungry to leave. He'd been so desperate to walk away from his family's market garden to something more exciting. Something that would bring him gold, like his grandfather had found in the mines.

He'd found his adventure on the *Terra Nova*. He'd become part of a team of explorers. He'd drawn so many amazing creatures with Wilson. He'd survived the winter journey to collect emperor penguin eggs. He'd been part of the support team for Captain Scott's expedition to the pole.

He'd already earned his money as a crew member. He could have collected it and taken it home to his family. His mother. He would have fulfilled his obligations to his whanau and made them proud. Wasn't that why he came in the first place? But he'd been too foolish to let go of the race. Too selfish. Too full of hero dreams.

And now he wouldn't help his mother or brothers. He wouldn't be a hero like his grandfather. He was going to freeze to death at the bottom of a crevasse. His family would never even know where he'd gone.

Jack's tears froze at the corners of his eyes. For a while, his anger at himself kept him awake. But now that he wasn't moving, it was cold. So cold.

It was so cold that he couldn't stop his body from shaking.

So cold that his twisted knee had stopped hurting.

And finally, it got so cold that it didn't feel cold anymore. So Jack lay down on the snow and closed his eyes. He was just feeling warm again when Ranger barked him awake.

• • •

"Hey there!"

"Sit up now!"

"Are you all right?"

"Jack!"

The men shouted down into the crevasse until Jack woke up and managed to get to his feet. The crevasse was forty or fifty feet deep, but they had plenty of rope. When they lowered it down with a harness, Jack tied a snug knot. Then he gave a tug on the rope, and the men hauled him up, and up, and up. Out of the darkness and back to hope.

Jack heard Ranger barking as the men were pulling him up. When he reached the top, he collapsed in a heap on the glacier. Ranger ran up and licked Jack's face as thankful tears spilled from his eyes. He was saved. He wasn't going to die alone at the bottom of the crevasse.

But now the stabbing cold had returned, and Jack felt it more than ever. He'd lost one of his skis and couldn't walk much with his twisted knee. The other men loaded him onto the sled and started back.

Jack had never been so happy to see the tent. Cherry helped Jack inside and held him steady while he changed out of his snowy outer clothes. Jack limped to his sleeping bag while the other men lit the stove. Ranger sat down beside Jack and licked the boy's face again.

Jack let out an exhausted, hoarse laugh. "You brought them to save me, didn't you, dog?" He gave Ranger a pat on the head. "I thought I wanted to go to the South Pole more than anything. But now, I —" The boy stopped talking and swallowed hard. "I just want to go home."

Ranger leaned in to Jack's hand and let the boy pet him some more. But then, Ranger heard a sound from the corner of the tent.

A quiet, high-pitched humming he hadn't heard in many long, cold months.

Ranger nuzzled Jack's fingers. Then he trotted to the corner of the tent. His first aid kit was there, half buried in a pile of pemmican cans, extra socks, and ropes. Ranger took the leather strap in his teeth and pulled the old metal box from the heap.

The humming grew louder. Ranger looked at the box. Then he went back to Jack, in his sleeping bag. Ranger gave the boy one more wet lick on his cheek.

"What's that for?" Jack laughed, wiping his face. "You know, dog, when Scott and the other men return, we'll board the *Terra Nova* to go home. You can live with me in New Zealand. We'll deliver potatoes to the greengrocers together!"

Ranger tipped his head and looked at the boy. He'd miss Jack Nin. But he'd been away from his other boy for so, so long. And Jack was going to be all right now, Ranger

could tell. It was time for both of them to go home.

Ranger sniffed at the sketchbook beside Jack's sleeping bag. He nosed at the pages until the book flopped open to the drawing Jack had made of Ranger on the ship so long ago.

Jack looked at Ranger. "You like that one, huh?" Then he reached over, tore the page from the sketchbook, folded up the picture, and tucked it under Ranger's collar. "You can keep it, okay? I'll put it up in the barn for you when we get home."

Home.

Ranger nuzzled the boy's hand. Then he went back to the first aid kit, took the strap in his teeth, and went to the door of the tent. He barked and pawed the way he did when he needed to go to the bathroom, and Cherry opened the tent to let him out.

Ranger dragged the old box out into the wind and snow. He could still hear the men cooking inside the tent. But the humming was getting louder. Light spilled from the cracks in the metal.

Ranger nuzzled the strap over his neck. The old first aid kit felt warm at his throat. Now he couldn't hear the tent noises anymore. The light grew brighter and brighter — brighter than the sun on Antarctica snow. So bright that Ranger had to close his eyes.

When he opened them, a piece of oatmeal cookie dropped to the floor in front of him.

Chapter 15

ADVENTURES IN THE SNOW

"There ya go, Ranger!" Luke pointed to the cookie piece with his foot. "You don't drink hot chocolate, but at least you can have a snack after a long afternoon in the snow."

Ranger scarfed up his treat. It wasn't a sledding biscuit. It was a real cookie. A *home* cookie!

"Whatcha got there?" Luke knelt down and pulled the folded-up paper from under Ranger's collar. He unfolded it and said, "Wow! That's pretty good. Sadie!" he called. "Did you draw this picture of Ranger?"

Sadie came and shook her head. "Maybe Noreen made it when she was here. She's really good in art class."

Ranger tipped his head up, took the corner of the drawing carefully in his teeth, and gently tugged it from Sadie's hands.

Luke laughed. "Don't worry, Ranger. We're not trying to take away your portrait. I'll put it up on your wall in the mudroom, okay?" Luke ran to the kitchen and came back with some tape. "How about right here over your dog bed?" He taped Jack's drawing to the wall and gave Ranger a scratch behind his ear. Then Luke and Sadie went back to their hot cocoa at the kitchen table.

Ranger climbed into his dog bed. He lowered his head and pawed away the strap of the first aid kit until the old metal box rested on his pillow. The box was quiet now.

And Ranger's blanket had never felt so wonderfully warm and dry. He curled up and looked at the drawing on the wall. The careful black and white pencil lines would always make him think of Jack, the boy who was so brave and hungry for adventure. Somehow, Ranger knew that Jack was warm and safe now, too.

"Hey, Ranger! You wanna go back outside and help us build a snow fort?" Luke called.

Ranger barked and stood up from his bed. He pawed his blanket over the first aid kit and the treasures from his other adventures. And he followed Luke back out into the snowy yard.

Home adventures were the best adventures of all.

Author's Note

Jack Nin is a fictional character, but his mixed Maori-Chinese cultural background is shared by many people in New Zealand today. Like Jack's grandfather, thousands of Chinese men came to work in the Otago goldfields in the 1860s to earn money for their families back in China. Some of those men went home after there was no more gold to be mined, but others stayed in New Zealand. Some raised families with native Maori women and became market gardeners, growing vegetables to sell. Many Chinese immigrants and their families faced discrimination from New Zealand people who complained that the immigrants were taking away jobs. Like Jack's family, children of these families learned English but held on to both their Chinese and Maori cultures as they worked long hours to earn a living. Today in New Zealand and around the world, descendants of these mixed families remember that heritage and take pride in their ancestry. The book *Being Maori Chinese: Mixed Identities* offers more insight on families like Jack's, and its author, Dr. Manying Ip, provided me with invaluable feedback about this part of the story.

There's no historical record of a boy sneaking onto the *Terra Nova*, but Jack's story is based on a real-life stowaway on Ernest Shackleton's *Endurance* in 1914. Perce Blackborow tried to get a job on the ship but was turned down, probably because he was young and didn't have experience. He managed to sneak onto the ship in Argentina and hide in a locker for three days before he got caught. A crew member wrote that Shackleton told the young man, "Do you know that on these expeditions we often get very hungry, and if there is a stowaway available he is the first to be eaten?"

Blackborow reportedly replied, "They'd get a lot more meat off you, sir." He was eventually hired as a steward for the voyage.

Other than Jack and Ranger, all of the crew members and animals mentioned in this story really did travel to Antarctica on board the *Terra Nova*, including Osman, the lead sled dog. Jack's adventures are based on real stories from history, documented in the journals, letters, and publications of the men who made the voyage. Many of these stories, including the killer whales, the dog-team crevasse rescue, the broken-up ice stranding, and the winter voyage to Cape Crozier with its blizzards and blown-away tent, are stories shared in detail in Apsley Cherry-Garrard's recollection of the polar voyage, *The Worst Journey in the World*.

When Captain Scott and his team set out for the final push to the South Pole, they understood that they might lose the race to Roald Amundsen, the Norwegian who'd gotten a better start and had more dogs for the trip. But they never gave up hope. Scott really did choose just four men to go with him for the last leg of the journey. They arrived at the South Pole on January 17, 1912, but could tell from a flag and tracks in the snow that Amundsen had beat them to the prize. Scott had lost the race, but the worst was yet to come.

The five men who made it to the pole — Robert Falcon Scott, Edgar Evans, Henry

"Birdie" Bowers, Edward "Uncle Bill" Wilson, and Lawrence "Titus" Oates — didn't have the happy endings that Jack did. On the way back to camp, the men encountered some of the worst conditions of the entire expedition. Evans had a cut thumb that wouldn't heal, along with terrible frostbite. He grew weaker and weaker and died on the return journey. Oates also had severe frostbite and an old leg wound that made it hard for him to keep up with the team. One day he walked out into a snowstorm and never returned to the tent.

The remaining three men were exhausted, weak, and running out of food when a blizzard stranded them for four days. Their next cache of supplies was just eleven miles away, but the storm trapped them in their tent. And then, they were too weak to go on.

Cherry-Garrard and the other men who'd returned to camp earlier had to wait for spring to go out and search for their friends. In November of 1912, they found the last camp and discovered their friends' bodies in the tent. They also found Captain Scott's diary. The final entry read:

Every day we have been ready to start for our depot 11 miles away, but outside the door of the tent it remains a scene of whirling drift. . . . We shall stick it out to the end, but we are getting weaker, of course, and the end cannot be far. It seems a pity, but I do not think I can write more.

R. Scott

Last Entry

For God's sake look after our people.

FURTHER READING

If you'd like to learn more about Scott's voyage, other Antarctic expeditions, and real-life working dogs like Ranger, check out the following books and websites:

Animals Robert Scott Saw: An Adventure in Antarctica by Sandra Markle (Chronicle Books, 2008)

Antarctica by Helen Cowcher (Square Fish, 2009)

DK Eyewitness Books: Arctic and Antarctic by Barbara Taylor (DK Publishing, 2012)

Shipwreck at the Bottom of the World: The Extraordinary True Story of Shackleton and the Endurance by Jennifer Armstrong (Knopf Books for Young Readers, 2000)

Sniffer Dogs: How Dogs (and Their Noses) Save the World by Nancy Castaldo (Houghton Mifflin Harcourt, 2014)

Trapped by the Ice!: Shackleton's Amazing Antarctic Adventure by Michael McCurdy (Walker, 2002)

Who Was Ernest Shackleton? by James Buckley (Grosset & Dunlap, 2013)

"Avalanche Rescue Dogs"

http://thebark.com/content/avalanche-rescue-dogs

"Meet the crew of Captain Robert Falcon Scott's Terra Nova Expedition"

https://www.nzaht.org/AHT/MeettheCrewEvans

"Scott's Last Expedition"

http://www.scottslastexpedition.org

SOURCES

The following books were also most helpful in my research:

American Rescue Dog Association. *Search and Rescue Dogs: Training the K-9 Hero.* Hoboken, NJ: Wiley Publishing, 2002.

Cherry-Garrard, Apsley. *The Worst Journey in the World* (Introduction by Caroline Alexander). New York: Penguin Books, 2005.

Ip, Manying. *Being Maori Chinese: Mixed Identities.* Auckland, NZ: Auckland University Press, 2008.

Jones, Max, Ed. *Robert Falcon Scott Journals: Captain Scott's Last Expedition.* Oxford: Oxford University Press, 2005.

MacPhee, Ross D. E. *Race to the End: Amundsen, Scott, and the Attainment of the South Pole.* New York: Sterling, 2010.

Parker, Steve. *Scott's Last Expedition.* London: Natural History Museum, 2011.

Savours, Ann, Ed. *Scott's Last Voyage: Through the Antarctic Camera of Herbert Ponting.* New York: Praeger Publishers, 1975.

Wilson, David M. *The Lost Photographs of Captain Scott: Unseen Images from the Legendary Antarctic Expedition.* New York: Little, Brown and Company, 2011.

ABOUT THE AUTHOR

Kate Messner is the author of *All the Answers*; *The Brilliant Fall of Gianna Z.*, recipient of the E. B. White Read Aloud Award for Older Readers; *Capture the Flag*, a Crystal Kite Award winner; *Over and Under the Snow*, a *New York Times* Notable Children's Book; and the Ranger in Time and Marty McGuire chapter book series. A former middle-school English teacher, Kate lives on Lake Champlain with her family and loves reading, walking in the woods, and traveling. Visit her online at www.katemessner.com.

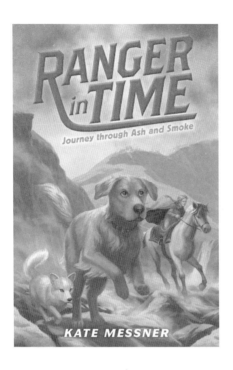

Ranger travels to Viking Age Iceland, where he meets Helga. When a nearby volcano erupts, Ranger and Helga must journey through ash and smoke, searching for her father. Helga discovers that too much courage can lead to big trouble, and ends up stranded on the edge of a crumbling cliff. Turn the page for a sneak peek!

"Where is Father?" Helga asked.

"Out chasing Rosta. That horse spooks so easily." Mother shook her head. "Your father had gone to see Ingar Olaffson about their property argument. But then the earth's trembling began and the horse took off running."

"I will go help Father search." Helga was good with the old horse and liked to remind her father that she was a good worker. So she tightened her cloak and started back out into the wind and rain.

She crossed the barley fields and wandered the shoreline. She climbed the gravel ridge that separated the lake from the sea and scanned the land in the distance.

But Helga could see neither her father nor his horse. She walked farther, to the vast fields of black rock and darkened tunnels. Perhaps Rosta was hiding in one of the larger caves.

The rain grew heavier. Jagged rocks poked

through Helga's shoes and scratched at the bottoms of her feet with every step.

"Rosta!" Helga slapped her hands on her knees. She made kiss sounds with her mouth, like she did when she brought the old horse food. But there was no sign of Rosta, and now rain poured from the sky.

Helga skipped from rock to rock over a rushing creek, slipping and sliding on the wet stones. "Father! Rosta!" she shouted.

Helga ducked under a stony bridge that spanned an area of soggy grass and ferns. Beyond that was a tunnel that had formed when old lava cooled. Helga crouched low and crawled into the sheltered dark to catch her breath.

The streams that flowed from the mountains were already rushing from the rain. Helga knew even from her short time in this land that too much water could sweep a person away. She would have to turn back. She hoped Father had found Rosta and was already on his way home.

Helga climbed back out into the blowing rain. She turned to where she thought the longhouse must be, but the clouds were so thick and low she couldn't see past the rocks in front of her. Helga turned, but the view was the same in every direction — walls of cloud and water, coming down faster than ever. Was her family's longhouse before her, or behind her?

The water puddled under Helga's feet. She couldn't see the stream that cut through a wide crevice in the rocks nearby, but she could hear it roaring.

"Father! Rosta!" she called.

But only the wind answered.